HELPER HOUNDS

Penny

Helps Portia Face Her Fears

HELPER HOUNDS

Penny

Helps Portia Face Her Fears

Caryn Rivadeneira
Illustrated by Priscilla Alpaugh

RED CHAIR
·PRESS·

Egremont, Massachusetts

RED CHAIR PRESS
BOOKS FOR YOUNG READERS

www.redchairpress.com

 Free educator's guide at www.redchairpress.com/free-resources

Publisher's Cataloging-In-Publication Data

Names: Rivadeneira, Caryn Dahlstrand, author. | Alpaugh, Priscilla, illustrator.

Title: Penny helps Portia face her fears / Caryn Rivadeneira ; illustrated by Priscilla Alpaugh.

Description: [Egremont, Massachusetts] : Red Chair Press, [2020] | Series: Helper hounds | Interest age level: 006-009. | Includes fun facts and information about the dog breed, American Pit Bull Terrier. | Summary: "Born with Down syndrome, Portia knows people want to limit what she can do. Inside herself, Portia knows she can do anything--including getting over her fear of dogs. But when Penny the pit bull terrier shows up, she isn't so sure."--Provided by publisher.

Identifiers: ISBN 9781634407755 (library hardcover) | ISBN 9781634407786 (paperback) | ISBN 9781634407816 (ebook)

Subjects: LCSH: American pit bull terrier--Juvenile fiction. | Down syndrome--Patients--Juvenile fiction. | Children with mental disabilities--Juvenile fiction. | Courage--Juvenile fiction. | CYAC: Pit bull terriers--Fiction. | Down syndrome--Patients--Fiction. | Courage--Fiction.

Classification: LCC PZ7.1.R5761 Pe 2020 (print) | LCC PZ7.1.R5761 (ebook) | DDC [E]--dc23

Library of Congress Control Number: 2019935133

Printed in Canada

0819 1P FRSP20

CHAPTER 1

The greyhounds huffed and chuffed. Their toenails clicked the cobblestone.

I knew these alleys like the pads of my paws. The Grey Sisters were fast, but they didn't know the twists and turns like I did. As long as I kept my head-start, the Grey Sisters would never catch me.

But those dogs were fast. After all, greyhounds were made to race. Now I was in a race for my... Well, I didn't know what the Grey Sisters wanted. I just knew they were scary, and I needed to get away.

I ran and ran. I turned and turned. I zipped

and zapped. My chest heaved. My legs launched my body forward.

Until I saw where I was. Just behind Mario's! I ducked behind the Dumpster. If I barked loud enough, Mario would hear me and answer the alley door. Maybe he'd bring me the steak burrito—extra hot—I was so crazy about.

I drooled just thinking about it. But I didn't have time to think! The Grey Sisters were getting closer. I could smell their bacon breath.

Bark! Bark! Bark!

Huff. Chuff.

Bark! Bark! Bark! Mario! Mario! Bark! Bark!

Huff. Huff. Chuff.

I froze. A snout poked into my butt. Oh no. A Grey Sister...

I growled but was too afraid to look. My body tensed. The hair along my spine stood straight up. I was ready to fight. But I hoped I wouldn't have to.

Poke. Poke. Poke.

Woof. Mario! Woof.

Poke. Poke. Giggle.

Wait. What?

Giggle. Giggle.

Poke. Shake.

Huh?

Poke. Pet. Pet.

Hold on...

I cracked open one eye. Then the other.

A girl with bushy hair like a squirrel's tail smiled at me.

Wait a minute. Where was I?

"Silly Penny," Hannah said.

Hannah! My tail thumped. I wasn't back in the alley after all. I was at the Mayfair House with the Helper Hounds!

CHAPTER 2

I stretched across the cool floor. My front pads landed on Sparkplug. He turned around fast and happy-barked in my face. I took two quick sniffs. Did Sparky have the bacon breath?

"You were drooling and barking in your sleep, Penny," Hannah said. She ran her hand down my back. "And your hair is standing up. Bad dream?" Hannah scrunched her red eyebrows at me.

It was nice of her to ask me about my dream. It *was* pretty scary. So I sat up and shook it off.

But I was at Mayfair House—in my bright red Helper Hounds vest—to help Hannah with *her* bad dreams!

Hannah had bad dreams. Really scary stuff. Hannah used to tell me about a big hairy monster that creeeeeeked the door open at night. Sometimes Hannah cried when she told me about the monster. When she did, I leaned in closer. I rested my big blocky head on her lap. And then Hannah would pet me. But sometimes—like this time—I dozed off.

Rude! I know! But just for a second. Hannah was such a good storyteller. She spoke low and slow. Plus, she was an even better petter. What could I do?

When I fell asleep, Hannah kept talking. And that's what I was there for—to listen to Hannah talk about monsters or anything else that worried her. But good news: lately Hannah's dreams had gotten much better. Sometimes she even dreamt about me!

"Did Penny fall asleep again, Hannah?" Miguel said.

Miguel! I sat up straighter and tilted my head toward Miguel. My tail hadn't stopped thumping since I woke up.

"She did, Mr. Miguel," Hannah said. "But that's okay. I pretend she's sleeping with me at night. So it's good practice when she does it for real."

Miguel laughed. "Well, I'm glad this lazy girl can help."

I slurped Hannah's hand. I was glad I could help too.

Miguel made small fists and brought his hands to his hips. This was the "here" command. I stood and took two steps toward Miguel. He clipped my Helper Hounds leash on.

"Well, time for us to go, Miss Hannah," Miguel said. "Sparky and Tasha should be leaving soon too. Penny will be back next week. Same time, same place?"

"Can't wait," Hannah said.

I couldn't either.

I licked Hannah goodbye. She hugged me, then waved as we left.

Miguel and I raced each other down the front staircase. I won. As always.

While Miguel caught his breath, he looked at his phone.

"Looks like we've got a new case, Penny," Miguel said. "A girl named Portia needs our help."

Then Miguel told me about Portia. Portia had done lots of hard things. Portia went to fourth grade even though some people didn't think she was smart enough. Portia played tennis and rode horses even though some people said she wasn't strong enough. Portia learned to do lots of things people never thought she could.

All because Portia had something called Down syndrome.

Portia was a champion at proving everyone wrong, Miguel said. But Portia still had one thing to conquer, one fear to face:

Portia was afraid of dogs!

And two new dogs had just moved into Portia's apartment building. Right downstairs! So Portia needed to get over her fear. And fast!

Most of the Helper Hounds would never understand how anyone could be afraid of dogs. But me? I get it. I used to be afraid of dogs too.

As Miguel told me more about Portia, I remembered my dream about the Grey Sisters. I shook.

My bad dream used to be my real life. Well, kind of.

CHAPTER 3

I wasn't scared of dogs when I was a puppy.

In fact, my brothers and sisters and I played very nicely, as I remember. Maybe only once or twice (okay, fifteen times a day), my mom had to dig her snout into the tumble of red-nosed pit bull puppies. Mom would grab one of us by the scruff to stop us from playing *too* hard.

The one getting grabbed was usually me. But what can I say? I'm a tough girl. I've never taken guff from any dogs—including my siblings.

But still, I don't remember them scaring me back then.

When I was old enough to start sleeping and

eating away from my mom, I went to live with a family with three human kids, a human mom, and one Chihuahua named Chip.

Chip hated me. And when I say hated, I mean *hated*. I tried to play but Chip would snarl and bark, growl and bite. I'd roll over to show Chip I knew he was boss. (Though, even as a puppy, I was much, much bigger than Chip.)

But Chip didn't care. Chip wanted me gone.

One day, the mom got tired of us fighting and chained me to a little shed in the backyard. Chip got to stay inside. The backyard wasn't so bad at first. I spent my days lying around the yard. I spied on squirrels as they scampered up trees. I darted out at bunnies as they munched clover. I liked the smells and sounds of the outside. The rumble of the train tracks near our house helped me go to sleep when the nights got lonely. And scary.

I didn't like hearing the howls and snarls of

other dogs. I wondered where they were and if they'd find me. And sometimes a raccoon would get a little *too* close to my crate. I'd bark and bark and hope to get let back in the house. Chip would look out the window. But no one ever opened the door.

Soon, they forgot about me altogether.

One day a neighbor boy heard me barking. He gave me a bowl of water and half of a peanut-butter and jelly sandwich. He pet my tummy and unclipped my chain when I got tangled in it. I hoped he would stay and play—forever—but when a woman called his name, the boy pet me one last time. Then ran out of the yard.

I took two giant steps after him. And then a forth and a fifth. I waited for my chain to tug at the collar around my neck. But it never did.

So I took a sixth and seventh and then an eighth step. The boy hadn't clipped me back up.

I was free! I started to run.

I ran and ran and ran. Then I trotted and trotted. And then I walked.

That's where I started my life on the streets and in the alleys. Good news: I wasn't on the streets or in the alleys very long. I only went through one season! Bad news: that season was a long Chicago winter. I spent most of my days looking for food and a warm place to sleep.

That's when I really became afraid of dogs! But that's also when I got a lot tougher. On the streets, you never know when a bigger, colder, or hungrier dog is going to try and take your food or your warm place to sleep. Rough-and-tumbling with my puppy siblings was one thing. Keeping the Grey Sisters from stealing my food and my blanket was another! I got so nervous around other dogs that I learned to bark and lunge first, ask questions later. And, the first time the Grey Sisters showed up and chased me through the alleys, my muscles tensed. My hair spiked. My barks got higher and higher until they sounded like screams. The Grey Sisters barked and snarled right back at me.

My friend Mario must have heard us in the alley. Before I knew it, a door squeaked open and a bucket of cold water splashed all around. The Grey Sisters took off. I curled behind the Dumpster and shook. Mario came out with a pile of dish towels, a bowl of water, and a steak burrito.

"You don't mind that the burrito fell on the floor, do you?" Mario said.

I didn't.

Mario waited while I scarfed down the steak from the burrito and spit out the beans. I lapped up the water. Then Mario toweled me off and scratched my neck.

My tail wagged and wagged. I loved Mario. I wanted him to be my human.

"Wish I could invite you into the restaurant, sweet girl," he said. "But no dogs allowed. The boss would fire me."

Mario piled the dish rags into a bed for me and walked back through the door.

Sounds sad, right? It was! But here's some good news: lots of people helped me. Mario fed me. Another lady opened her garage for me and piled blankets for me to sleep on. One man bent to scratch me every single day. Sometimes he even had a treat!

But still no one invited me into their cars or homes or lives, until one day, a car slowed as I trotted through the snow.

"Hey, puppy," a voice said through the open window. I wasn't much of a puppy anymore, but I didn't care. The voice sounded nice. My tail wagged.

The car pulled along the curb. I sat in a pile of snow and watched as the car came to a stop.

The man with the nice voice got out and said: "You lost, pup?"

I wasn't really lost. But the voice was so nice that I wagged and wagged. The man walked up slowly and then knelt in front of me. He held out his hand. I sniffed it.

His hand smelled like food so I licked it. Then I moved in to kiss his face. The man laughed and fell back in the snow. I wiggled and wagged and licked his whole face.

I fell right in love.

The man sat up and scratched my back.

Then he snuck a long leash around my neck. It felt weird at first, like my old chain. So I shook and tried to wiggle it off. But when he stood up, slapped his leg, and invited me to follow, I did. And when he opened the car door and patted the seat, I jumped right in. I curled up and snuggled down on the front seat. The car was warm and soft and smelled like fried chicken. I was tired.

The man laughed when he sat down next to me. He scratched my neck and as I was drifting off, I heard him say: "I'm Miguel. But who are you, sweetie? Where are you from?"

I didn't know how to answer either of those questions so I just fell asleep as the car rumbled on.

Next thing I knew, the car stopped.

"We're home," Miguel said.

CHAPTER 4

While I lapped up water and then gobbled down some chopped-up chicken in Miguel's kitchen, Miguel called the police station and the animal shelters.

"She's a penny-colored pit bull," he'd say into his phone. "No collar. Real skinny."

Then Miguel would come back to me, scratch my ears, and say: "Doesn't sound like anyone is missing you, pup."

This was not news to me. I would have told Miguel this, but we didn't speak the same language yet.

And so I stayed that night—with Miguel. He gave me a bath, brushed my hair, and let me sleep right on his bed. As I fell asleep, Miguel scratched my neck and called me "Penny." I liked the way he said that. Penny was a good name. I rested my snout on his chest. That's all I remember of that first night.

The next day Miguel's sister, Elisa, came by with some dog food, a real leash, and a big bed. Elisa is a vet—an animal doctor. Normally she works with elephants and tigers and huge snakes (*yuck*) at the zoo. But she knows lots about dogs too. So Elisa looked at my teeth, clipped my toenails, ran a little comb through my hair, and poked me with a needle. I didn't like it, but Elisa told me I was a good girl. A *very* good girl.

"I can't believe she's so trusting," Elisa said. "Looks like she was homeless for a long time. She's so calm."

Miguel nodded.

"She's a quick learner too," Miguel said. "Penny can already sit. Basic commands won't be a problem. Penny could be great."

I had no idea what they thought I'd be great at, but I liked hearing "Penny." And I liked the treats Elisa and Miguel gave me every time I sat and when I slid down to the floor.

"Alright," Elisa said as she scratched my neck. "Let's see how she is with Tex."

That's when things got tricky.

Miguel clipped a leash on my brand new collar and said, "Sit." I sat. A door opened. Next thing I knew, a huge German shepherd was tapping his nails across Miguel's floor. Hair flew from his slinky body.

Tex woof-woof-woofed when he saw me.

My body tensed. The hair along my spine spiked.

I was terrified. He was even bigger than a

Grey Sister! He might try to take my bed, my new home, my food!

The rest is a bit of a blur.

I lunged at Tex. I didn't even bark. I just pulled hard against the leash. Tex just kept swiffing his tail back and forth. He wasn't afraid at all.

Miguel called my name and told me to sit. I did. But I kept my eyes on Tex. Then Miguel made a clicky sound with his mouth. When I looked up at him, he gave me a bit of liver. Yum!

I looked back at Tex. Miguel clicked again so I looked back at Miguel. More liver! Yum again! This was fun.

My body relaxed. If looking away from Tex was going to get me liver treats, Tex could stay all day.

"That's good. She's relaxing," Elisa said. "But she'll have to keep working on her 'dog reactivity.'"

I had no idea what "dog reactivity" was but again: if working on it meant more treats, I was all in.

Long story short: Elisa and Tex started coming by every day. (Well, except for the week after I got my little operation to make sure I wouldn't have puppies. Don't worry: that wasn't so bad. I got extra snuggles and treats!)

Then, before I knew it, I would greet Tex without barking or lunging. Now my tail wagged and we could romp and stomp and play with my alligator tug toy. I even learned how to eat out of bowl right next to Tex without getting nervous.

I still had trouble with some of the dogs I met at the dog-food store and that one crazy poodle at the vet. But most dogs didn't seem so scary anymore. In fact, I began to wonder what I'd been afraid of all along.

But then sometimes, I'd dream about the Grey Sisters and it would all come back to me. I'd shake and rumble in my sleep, but I'd wake up to Miguel smiling at me and telling me what a good girl I was. Then I remembered: I was home and I was safe.

All this time, Miguel and I practiced our commands. I got really good at "sit," "down," "stay," "leave it," "here," "come," "settle," "sit pretty," even "roll over." And I got very popular with the kids in the neighborhood. Miguel took me for lots of walks and gave me extra pats when I sat nicely and took treats softly from the kids who always came out to pet me.

Miguel and I also went to special training classes with other dogs. I did really well. On the last night of the class, I sat still as a statue while kids and dogs ran past me, then a lady in a wheelchair zoomed by, and balloons popped and bottles dropped all around me. I got my

Canine Good Citizen badge that night. Miguel game me lots of extra treats and hugs.

Then one day Miguel found me leaning against our fence. Melanie, the girl next door, was crying on the other side. I was just trying to listen—and to let her know I would listen. Miguel ran to get his phone. He recorded me as I shifted so Melanie could reach good places to pet me and as I snuck my paw through the fence so she could hold it.

Miguel texted the picture to his sister.

"I knew you were something special the day I saw you wandering in the snow," Miguel said to me after Elisa texted back.

That was nice to hear. I thought Miguel was something special that day too.

CHAPTER 5

Two days later, Elisa and Tex came over with a man named Mr. Tuttle. He was the head trainer for the Helper Hounds. Every summer, Mr. Tuttle and some of the Helper Hounds taught a summer camp for kids at the zoo where Elisa worked.

That was the first time I ever heard of Helper Hounds. I was still just a dog from the streets, learning new things every day. And that day, I learned all about Helper Hounds. I also learned that as head trainer, Mr. Tuttle decided which dogs got to go to Helper Hounds University, and then which dogs got to graduate and become actual Helper Hounds.

I could tell from Miguel's jittery hands and jittery laugh that Mr. Tuttle was important.

Good news: When you have relied on the kindness of strangers most of your life like I did, everyone is important and you treat everybody that way. So, "important" people never make me nervous.

I went right up and licked Mr. Tuttle's hand hello. When he said "sit," I sat. When he motioned for me to "come," I came. When he put me in a stay and started doing jumping jacks, I tilted my head at the weird man, but I stayed put.

Mr. Tuttle said I was a very good girl.

"I heard other dogs could be a problem with her," Mr. Tuttle said while watching me and Tex sniff each other's behinds.

"They were at first," Miguel said. "Who knows what she had to deal with on the street. But Penny has relaxed now. I wouldn't apply if I thought dog aggression was an issue."

Miguel's voice came out higher than normal. Still nervous, I guess.

"She does seem fine with Tex," Mr. Tuttle said. "Elisa? What do you think?"

While Elisa talked about my finer points, about how *calm* I was around people and how relaxed kids were around me, I decided to give myself a bit of a bath. I sat and stretched my back leg high in the air. That's the best way to freshen the leg pits. But I must've stretched a little *too* high because before I knew it, I tumbled back. Right onto Tex.

Tex had been freshening up himself. So he didn't see me coming at all. As soon as my body hit his, his head jerked back and his upper lip pulled back. He showed me all his teeth. I have to admit: It was scary. Miguel, Elisa, and Mr. Tuttle stopped talking. All eyes turned on us.

But Miguel had taught me well. I looked

right at Miguel and picked myself up. Tex just went back to licking.

"Impressive," Mr. Tuttle said. "She is definitely relaxed."

Mr. Tuttle knelt down next to me. "Congratulations, Ms. Penny," Mr. Tuttle said. "We look forward to seeing you next semester at Helper Hounds University."

Elisa said, "Yay!" And Miguel got down to hug me.

I just kept on with my bath.

Long story short: Helper Hounds University was a lot of fun. I learned lots of new tricks and got lots of treats. Most of them for just lying around. We visited schools and hospitals. We flew on airplanes and rode on trains. We went up elevators and down escalators. We met cats and horses and lots and lots of people.

Other dogs won awards for sitting the quickest or staying the longest. My only award was for the best "settle." I'd settle so well, I'd fall asleep. I still do, as you know. It's a gift.

Anyway, I graduated at the end of the semester and got my red vest, my red leash, and my ID card. From street dog to Helper Hound in less than a year. What a life!

But now, let's get back to Portia.

CHAPTER 6

Portia's neighborhood looked a lot like ours.
Rows of three-family-flats lined the block. Every
once in a while, a single-family home snuck in.
Some were bungalows like the one Miguel and I
lived in. Others were tall thin "Victorians" with
front porches and loopy woodwork. Miguel
called those houses "Gingerbread." It sounded
yummy. I hoped Portia lived in one of those.
But instead, we pulled up in front of a gray,
stone "three-flat" with bulging bay windows
and a steep front stoop. The roof looked like
a crown. Miguel called it a "parapet," which
sounded fun.

People must've known we were coming. As soon as Miguel turned off the engine, kids ran toward the car.

"Portia!" a boy yelled. "The Helper Hounds are here!"

I put my front feet on the window and wagged my tail—right into Miguel's face—as he reached to straighten my vest and grab our backpack.

Miguel grabbed my leash and I followed him out his door. The kids formed a semi-circle as we approached.

They all smiled at me. I smiled back. My tail wagged and wagged.

"Can we pet her?" a boy asked.

"Sure," Miguel said. "Just don't crowd her. Penny doesn't really mind. But lots of dogs hate that."

A few of them gathered around and pet me hello. Miguel pointed out the best places on my back to pet me.

"Thanks for the warm welcome," Miguel said. "This is Penny."

"We know," another girl said. "We saw her picture online. She was at that fire."

"That's right," Miguel said. "Penny and a few of her friends from Helper Hounds University hung out with some folks after their apartment building burned down. It was really sad. Penny was glad to help."

The kids pet and pet and pet me. I rolled over so they could scratch my belly. That made one little girl giggle non-stop.

"I hate to interrupt all the love," Miguel said.

"But we're here to see Portia. Are any of you Portia?"

Miguel smiled and scanned the crowd. I sat up and did the same. My tail swept the sidewalk.

The kids stepped back and pointed. One girl stood on the front walk. Her hands dug deep into her pockets. The girl looked up at a woman who leaned against a huge cement planter at the top of the stoop. The woman smiled and nodded at Portia.

Portia pulled a hand from her pocket and waved. "I'm Portia," she said.

I stood up. My tail sliced the air.

Miguel walked us forward a few steps. Portia froze—straighter than the parapet above her. Miguel told me to sit. So I did.

The woman at the top of the stoop hopped down the stairs, her hand straight out.

"Pleasure to meet you," she said. "I'm Nance Obello Tornsten. Portia's mother."

Miguel shook Nance's hand. "I'm Miguel,"
he said. "And this is Penny." Miguel turned to
Portia. "Would you like to pet her hello?"

"No, thank you," Portia said. "Not yet."

Miguel laughed and said, "Fair enough!"

Portia's mom suggested we wave goodbye
to the audience of kids and head into the
backyard.

"Great idea!" said Miguel. I barked my
agreement.

Miguel waved goodbye, I gave the giggly

girl a quick lick, and then we headed down the alleyway between the three-flats. I used to hang out in places like this when I lived outside. You'd be surprised how cozy a spot between two garbage cans and a warm brick wall could be! But I was glad to be walking through—and not snuggling in for the night.

Nance opened the gate for us and we all walked through. Penny and Nance first, then Miguel and me.

I stopped for a sniff of the yard: possum poop, roses, grilled steaks, and something else, another smell—bacon-y—that was familiar, but I couldn't quite place. It didn't matter: I didn't like rose bushes much (ouch!), but possum poop and grilled steaks made every backyard better!

I looked at Portia. I wondered if she liked the possum poop smell too.

Portia stared at me. I relaxed my big face into a smile. I hoped she'd relax too. But she held her eyes tight on mine.

"Let's sit," Nance said. She waved her hand toward the backyard furniture. Nance and Portia sat on one set. I climbed up next to Miguel on the other.

"Oh, sorry," Miguel said. "Is this okay?"

Nance laughed and said, "Be my guest!" I curled up for a snooze.

"Penny's a pit bull," Portia said.

"She is!" Miguel said. "Well, as far as we know, at least..."

"Pit bulls are mean," Portia said.

I opened one eye. Then lifted my head. If I had a steak for every time Miguel and I heard people say pit bulls were mean, I'd weigh a lot more than my fifty pounds.

"Why do you say that?" Miguel asked.

"I've seen stories about them," Portia said. "In the news."

"Pit bulls do get in the news," Miguel said.

"It seems like any time a dog bites, it's a pit bull, right?"

Portia nodded.

"I know from your mom, your teacher, and the way you ask questions that you're one smart girl," Miguel said. "So I'm going to give you the straight-up facts, okay, *amiga*?"

"Okay," Portia said.

"Pit bulls get *written about* in the news more than other dogs, but that doesn't mean they *bite* more than any other dogs," Miguel said. "In fact, Google it! No dog breed or type bites more than any other. Not pit bulls. Not rottweilers. Not German shepherds. Not poodles. Not pot roast and noodles."

Miguel smiled. Portia laughed.

"If Dr. Seuss wrote about dog bites…" Nance said.

"But for some reason, pit bulls make good headlines," Miguel said. "And people get scared.

Just because they don't understand. They think Penny's mean without even getting to know her. Pit bulls are misunderstood."

Portia's eyes drifted over to me. Her eyes were softer now. I sat up and wagged. Portia smiled at me. Just for a second.

"I'm misunderstood," said Portia.

"How so?" Miguel asked.

"People look at me and think I can't read or can't ride horses," Portia said. "They think I'm not smart or strong enough."

"And are they right?" Miguel said.

"No way," said Portia. "I'm strong and I'm smart no matter what anyone thinks."

"Same with Penny," Miguel said. "She—along with most pit bulls I've ever met—are sweet and silly and sleepy no matter what anyone else thinks! You'll see once you get to know her. And you'll see your new neighbor dogs aren't so bad when you get to know them too!"

Portia's mom squeezed her arm around Portia. "What happens when they get to know you, hon'?"

Portia laughed. "They invite me to book club and get jealous of my blue ribbons."

"Well done," Miguel said. He put out his fist. Portia bumped it.

"Would you like to learn about dogs?" Miguel asked. "And then get to know Penny?"

Portia nodded. "I don't want to be afraid of dogs any more," she said. "I want to understand them."

"And that, *amiga*, is the first step in getting over your fear," Miguel said. "*Muy bien!*"

CHAPTER 7

I curled up on the wicker sofa and caught semi-snoozes while Miguel told Portia all about dogs. And I mean *all* about dogs. Miguel went back 10,000 years. All the way back to the one friendly wolf that wandered up to a human's campfire. Miguel told how that friendly wolf's friendly puppies had other friendly puppies and on and on until: *voila*! Dogs!

Miguel talked about breeding—and *over-breeding*—and about all the dogs who live (and die…) in shelters. Miguel talked about our teeth and jaws. Miguel gave the speech on how pit bulls' jaws do not "lock" like some people say.

I opened one eye as Miguel pulled my mouth open and said, "See?" Portia nodded. Then she smiled at me. We were making progress!

I snoozed on as Miguel told Portia about how we like to be pet—and how we don't. He said we don't like staring contests (staring makes us nervous) and how when you run, we will chase. And dogs are faster than humans. So we'll catch you! Much better to make like a tree and stand very still. Speak nicely! We like baby talk. It calms us right down.

But Miguel also warned never to go up to a strange dog—especially not when it's tied up, eating, or chewing a bone or toy.

And then Miguel talked about dog bites.

"Most of the time," Miguel said, "dogs don't bite because they're 'bad'—they do it because they're scared or because they've been mistreated. Sometimes it's because people don't know how to *read a dog*."

And it's true. Lots of people don't!

"But you're a great reader," Miguel said. "Of people and horses and books. So learning to read dog should be no problem."

Portia nodded.

"Are you ready to see how nice dogs can be?" Miguel asked. Portia nodded again.

Then it was time to put everything Portia learned into practice. Miguel shook me awake. I jumped down onto the grass. Portia held out her hand.

CHAPTER 8

I went all wiggly. Wiggly neck. Wiggly butt. Wiggly walk. I took two quick sniffs of Portia's hands but I already knew she was good.

"See Penny's body language?" Miguel asked. Penny nodded. "That's how you know a dog is happy to see you. She's wiggly and loose. Now, let's review the rules. Do you remember?"

Portia nodded and began to recite: "Relax and walk up to the dog carefully. Not too fast. Not too slow. Don't stare. Don't bend down. Don't hug. Don't wave your arms or jump around. Be polite."

Miguel laughed. "Great memory!" he said.

"Go for it. And after she sniffs your hand, tell her to sit."

Miguel handed Portia a treat. Portia took a deep breath and looked at me. Then she looked away quickly. Her eyes raced across the backyard—looking at everything BUT me.

"Great job, Portia," Miguel said. "You can look at her. Just don't stare at her face."

"Okay," Portia said. She breathed in and out, in and out, peanut butter and jelly on her breath. Yum! Then she took one big breath and said, "Sit!"

I sat.

"Hand her the treat," Miguel said.

Portia reached forward—slowly, slowly— with the bit of liver snack. I leaned forward and started to open my mouth when—zap! Portia whipped her hand back.

Somewhere in my brain, the deep-down wolf in me wanted to snap at the treat and see if I could snatch it out of her hand. I didn't. But not all dogs have my self-control!

"You did great," Miguel said. "But let's try that again. And let's add 'Don't yank your hand away' to the list, okay? Penny knows how to take a treat nicely. You don't have to be scared of her mouth."

Portia reached her hand forward again and opened her palm. The bit of liver sat right in the middle. I leaned forward and reached out my lips forward. *Voila*! Liver in my mouth!

I sat up and wiggled some more. Portia laughed.

"Good girl," Nance said from the chair. "Tell her she's a good girl too, Portia."

"Good girl," Portia said. Almost like she meant it. "I want to try it again."

Miguel handed Portia more treats. Before she knew it, Portia was taking me through all my tricks. I went down. I stayed. I sat pretty and rolled over. This time, Portia met me on the lawn to give me my treat—and a belly rub.

"You *are* a good girl!" Portia said. "She's not wild like the sisters."

"The sisters?" Miguel asked.

"The dogs that live downstairs," Nance said. "They get jumpy. That's what Portia's really afraid of."

"Ah," Miguel said. "Well, Penny's not much of a jumper, but I can give you some tips. But you have to stand up."

Portia gave my belly one last scratch. I flipped over to watch.

"If a dog jumps," Miguel said, "you go stiff and tall like a tree again. But this time, you bring your hands up and together. Like you're praying, but close to the chest."

Portia mimicked Miguel. Portia's mom stood up to try it too.

"Then," Miguel said, "you turn away. A

jumping dog just wants your attention. But jumping on people is rude. And even little dogs can knock people over! So we don't want to reward jumping with attention."

Portia and Miguel ran through the motions together. They looked like dancers. I strolled over for a closer look. Portia had it down pat. Like she'd been working with dogs her whole life. I poked my snout into her knee to let her know she was great.

Portia bent down to pet me. I licked her hand and she didn't yank it back. Then I sat down. She followed and asked Miguel if she could give me a hug.

Miguel said yes. "But not too hard, not too tight, and not too long," he said. "Penny doesn't mind being snuggled but *most* dogs are not fans of tight hugs."

Portia hugged me just the right amount and then told me I was a good girl. I barked to let her know she was good too.

"I don't feel afraid anymore!" Portia said. Her mom and Miguel applauded. Portia stood up and laughed.

"Time to try your new skills out on some other dogs?" Miguel asked.

Portia nodded.

"I'll go get the sisters," Nance said.

"Great," said Miguel. "We'll just play some fetch while we wait for the girls."

My third time bringing the stick back to Portia, I paused to sniff that bacon-y smell again. It was so familiar. I sniffed again. My memory was becoming clearer...I could almost place it...And then, the "girls" arrived on the back porch.

I stood stock still. The hair along my spine spiked. I began to shake.

The Grey Sisters stared down at me from the back deck.

CHAPTER 9

Portia was the first to notice. She walked over and put her hand on my vest. Portia shook too.

"Penny," she said. "That's Grey Goose and Grey Duck. You don't have to be afraid. Remember the rules?"

I did. I remembered the rules. So I looked at Miguel. But there was no treat. He was talking to Nance and their human neighbors. But of course, Miguel wasn't worried about me. The Grey Sisters were on leashes. I was a well-trained, world famous Helper Hound! Plus, it had been years since another dog scared me.

Then again, it had been years since the Grey

Sisters chased me. I tried to relax, but when the
one sister—Grey Goose, I think—locked her
eyes on mine, I worked hard not to lunge.

Portia knelt beside me. "Penny, see Grey
Goose and Grey Duck? See how they wiggle?
They're happy to see you!"

I bet they were! After all these years, the
Grey Sisters finally had the chance to dig their
claws and teeth into me and to steal my food
and blankets!

"Now, we need to relax and walk up to the dogs carefully. Not too fast. Not too slow," Portia said. Portia clicked her tongue. I looked right up at her. She returned my attention with a "Good girl."

"Don't stare at the dogs, Penny," Portia said. "And when we say hello, don't hug them. Don't wave your arms like a wild girl. Be polite."

Portia patted my vest and leaned against me. She picked up my leash.

I looked up at Portia and smiled. She was right. We had nothing to be afraid of! Dogs weren't scary! So I took one big step forward. Then another and another. Portia held my leash all the way to the bottom of the back porch, where Miguel talked to two men standing next to the Grey Sisters.

"You won't believe this, Penny!" Miguel said as he hopped down to meet me. "Grey Duck and Grey Goose were found wandering lost right where you used to live. They got adopted by these guys not long after I found you. What are the chances?"

I wished the chances were zero. But here we were: finally ready to meet. Not in some back alley. Not behind a Dumpster at Mario's. But in this nice backyard surrounded by people who loved us and took care of us and one girl who needed to see dogs weren't so scary.

So as the Grey Sisters hustled down the back steps on their leashes, I sat. My tail wagged. My mouth sagged into a dopey smile.

The Sisters sat in front of me too. Then we got the "okay" to sniff each other, which we did. Nicely. Grey Goose stuck her snout a little further in my ear than I normally would like. But I just shook it off and then I put my head over her neck. Just because. Funny: I'd never noticed that I could even do that if I stood tall.

"Glad to see you girls getting on so

well," Miguel said. "But we're here for Portia, remember?" Then Miguel clicked his tongue and walked me back to the furniture. I sat next to him while the Grey Sisters sat in front of Portia.

You should've seen her. Portia silently mouthed all the rules as she walked up to the dogs. She held out her hand and then gave small scratches on the back. When Grey Duck jumped up, Portia pulled her hands into prayer and spun like a ballerina. Grey Duck lost her balance and toppled to the ground. It was pretty funny.

Soon we were all let off our leashes and allowed to chase each other around the yard a bit. Funny thing: greyhounds are fast—faster than I'll ever be—but they get tired even faster! They were asleep before I was.

I bet that day Portia never imagined she'd end up snuggled up between three snoozing dogs in her backyard. For sure, I never imagined I'd be snuggled up with the Grey Sisters, and a brave

girl named Portia. Life is funny that way. It's always great to make new friends—especially when those friends used to be enemies.

And I realized—snoozing there on the deck—that sometimes our dreams are scary. But that doesn't mean the monsters will always be monsters. I'd have to find a way to tell Hannah that when I visit her again next week.

EPILOGUE

Dear Penny:

Looked like you loved Grey Duck and Grey Goose a lot. So I'm sending you their picture. I also drew one of all of us on the blanket in the backyard. Before Grey Duck peed on it. LOL

I'm not afraid of dogs now. Well, except this beagle that lives near school. I don't like how he barks in the window. Maybe Miguel can help me with that? I just run past the house, but I don't think that's what I'm supposed to do.

I hope you come back to visit. Mom said she wants to invite all the Hounds to come help the kids read at school. I'd love that. Hope you would too.

Your friend,

Portia

Miguel's
Never-Fear Dog Tips

Watch Their Language

Most dogs are nice and friendly. But when a dog isn't friendly, it's usually because they are scared—not mean! You can tell if a dog is nervous or afraid (a) if they stand stiff, (b) if they lock their eyes on you, (c) if they hold their tails still or wag slowly, or (d) if they growl or bark and lunge at you.

When a dog is friendly and unafraid, its body is loose and wiggly. And most barking is friendly barking. You can see that it's relaxed.

Obey the Growl

A growl is just a warning! So never yell at a dog for growling at you. The dog is trying to tell you to go away or STOP doing what you're doing. So when a dog growls, listen. Stop what you're doing and move away.

Mind Your Manners

Never rush up to a dog or smother it with hugs—whether it's a dog you know or don't know. Most dogs don't like to be overwhelmed. They feel trapped. Just like us!

Give Them Space

Dogs like space to eat and play. Sometimes they need to be alone—just like humans! So when a dog is eating or chewing a bone, let it be. And don't pet a strange dog through a fence. That's their yard! They might feel protective.

Don't Stare

Dogs don't love to be stared at. I don't either! So while it's great to look at a dog—don't glue your eyes onto its.

Be a Tree

If a dog chases you, don't run. Instead, be a tree! You can always yell "Go home" or "Go away." But usually if you stand still long enough, the dog will lose interest. If a dog knocks you over and you feel afraid, curl into a tight ball. Cover your face with your hands or arms.

Be Nice

Most dogs are nice. Just like most people are nice! The nicer you are to dogs, the nicer they'll be to you. Of course, the beautiful thing about most dogs—including so many dogs at the shelters now—is that dogs are the most forgiving creatures on Earth. Some people are mean to dogs, but dogs still keep treating us like kings and queens. They need us to be kind to them.

FUN FACTS

About Pit Bulls

In this story, Penny is a super-sweet dog. Most pit bulls are. Unfortunately, these dogs have a bad reputation. Some people think they are vicious and likely to bite. Many people are afraid of pit bulls. But as Penny shows us, pit bulls are not scary at all. They are usually big bundles of love!

Pit bulls are not an actual breed, like a German Shepard or a Dachshund. The name "pit bull" is used in broad terms for a large group of dogs. In the United States, this group includes the pit bull terrier, the Staffordshire bull terrier, and the American Staffordshire terrier.

Hundreds of years ago, people in England bred bulldogs and terriers to create a breed of fighting dog. Pit bulls are strong and stocky. They have big heads and powerful jaws. Back in the 1200s, people paid to see fights between these dogs and bigger animals, like bears or bulls. These fights were held in deep, open spaces called pits. That's how the term pit bull got started.

By the 1800s, fights between dogs, bears, and bulls were against the law. So people started fighting dogs against each other instead. The pit bull was one of the most popular breeds for dog fighting. Sadly, this is still true today.

This violent history is why pit bulls get such a bad rap. However, pit bulls are not born to be bad. Instead, they usually fight only if their owners force them. Those owners are the real bad guys! And dog fighting is now against the law in all US states.

In fact, at one time, pit bulls were favorite family pets. They were even movie stars. A pit bull named Petey appeared in many popular movies as part of the Little Rascals gang. In World War I, pit bulls were used as a symbol for the United States. The dog was seen as strong, loyal, and brave, just like the American soldiers.

Other famous pitties, as they are sometimes called, are Nipper, the mascot of RCA television, and Tige, the mascot for Buster Brown shoes. And you've probably seen advertisements for Target stores featuring a miniature pit bull named Bullseye.

Pit bulls do have a bad reputation, it's true. But the idea that all pit bulls are dangerous is fading. These dogs can be great family pets. Some, like Penny, are emotional support dogs. Just like all dogs, pit bulls need to be trained to be good doggie citizens. That's a smart idea, because these tough-looking dogs are just big bundles of cuddly love!